WELCOME TO

Beast Quest®

W9-BRJ-734

Collect the special coins in this book.
You will earn one gold coin for
every chapter you read.

Once you have finished all the chapters,
find out what to do with your gold coins at
the back of the book.

With special thanks to Lucy Courtenay

For my very own Beasts, Alfie and George

www.beastquest.co.uk

ORCHARD BOOKS
Carmelite House
50 Victoria Embankment
London EC4Y 0DZ

A Paperback Original
First published in Great Britain in 2007
This edition published in 2015

Beast Quest is a registered trademark of Beast Quest Limited
Series created by Beast Quest Limited, London

A CIP catalogue record for this book is available from
the British Library.

ISBN 978 1 84616 989 2

28

Printed and bound by CPI Group (UK) Ltd, Croydon, CR0 4YY

The paper and board used in this book are made from wood
from responsible sources.

Orchard Books
An imprint of Hachette Children's Group
Part of The Watts Publishing Group Limited
An Hachette UK Company

www.hachette.co.uk

Beast Quest®

Claw
THE GIANT
MONKEY

BY ADAM BLADE

ORCHARD

WESTERN OCEAN

THE FOREST
OF FEAR

THE RUBY DESERT

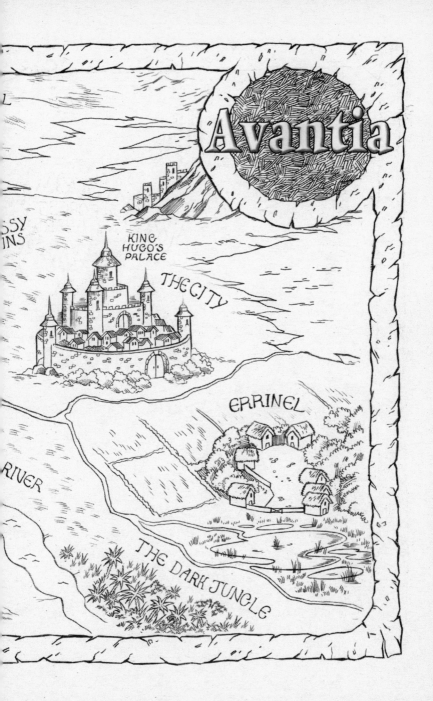

CONTENTS

Did you think it was over?

Did you think I would accept defeat, and disappear?

No! That can never be. I am Malvel, the Dark Wizard who strikes fear into the hearts of the people of Avantia. I still have much more to show this kingdom, and one boy in particular...Tom.

The young hero liberated the six Beasts of Avantia from my curse. But his fight is far from over. Let us see how he fares with a new Quest, one that will surely crush him and his companion, Elenna.

Avantia's Beasts had good hearts that I corrupted for my own wicked purpose. Now, thanks to Tom, they are free to protect the kingdom once more. But now I bring to Avantia six Beasts whose hearts are evil and so cannot be set free: monster squid, giant monkey, stone charmer, snake man, king of spiders and three-headed lion. Each one guards a piece of the most precious relic of Avantia, which I have stolen: the suit of Golden Armour that gives magical strengths to its rightful owner. I will stop at nothing to prevent Tom collecting the complete suit and defeating me again. This time he will not win!

Malvel

PROLOGUE

The air was hot and humid. The market trader mopped his brow and stared into the thick mass of jungle trees before him. It reminded him of rotten black teeth. Heavy vines hung down like snakes.

"Do we have to go there?" asked the boy at the trader's side. "Is there no other way?"

"We've travelled for days for

the Ruby Guya fruit," the trader
reminded his assistant. "It grows
nowhere else in Avantia. Only here
in the Dark Jungle."

"But aren't there monsters who
live here? That's what people say,"
the boy whispered.

Everyone in Avantia knew
the terrors of the Dark Jungle:

creatures that plucked men from the ground and ate them whole; plants whose rich scents could overwhelm a person at twenty paces. Few dared to enter – and fewer still returned.

"Rumours to frighten honest men," said the trader with a wave of his hand.

"Is it true the Ruby Guya possesses miraculous powers?" the boy asked.

The trader nodded. "One bite of its sweet red flesh brings courage to the faint-hearted and strength to the weak," he said. "It is only ever seen at the king's table, and fetches a price beyond gold." He glanced at his young assistant.

"But we must keep our heads if we are to harvest it. Do you understand?"

The boy swallowed his fear and nodded.

They entered the jungle side by side. At once the light grew dim. The ground was marshy beneath their feet and there was a stench of rotting vegetation. Birds screamed and wheeled overhead. Great tree ferns arched above them, their leaves a bright and poisonous green.

The trader gazed at the fleshy jungle flowers that hung in ropes from the trees. They smelled overripe and dangerous. He forced all thoughts of creatures and deadly scents from his mind. But he couldn't shake the feeling that something was watching them.

A branch crashed to the ground. The trader whirled, pulling his knife from its sheath in one swift movement. But all he saw were shadows.

They walked on. Soon they found themselves wading through a foul smelling swamp. The thick, pungent water lapped at their knees. The trader clenched his teeth to stop himself from trembling. Who knew what vile creatures lurked at his feet?

He wanted to weep with relief when they touched solid ground again.

"We must press on," he said.

The boy crawled out of the swamp. "Leeches," he sobbed. "They're all over my legs!"

The trader prised the leeches from the boy's bare ankles with the blade of his knife. Shuddering, he did the same to the bloodsuckers on his own limbs. The Dark Jungle was a terrible, stinking place. He would be glad to leave – once he had found the fruit he sought.

They moved on. Shafts of sunlight seemed to drip to the ground like venom. Monkeys chattered in the highest treetops above them. It sounded as if they were laughing.

At last, through the ferns, the trader glimpsed a cluster of trees with green, waxy leaves and plump red fruits. His heart leapt.

The Ruby Guya!

The trader hauled himself into the nearest tree, laughing with delight.

"Come on, boy!" he called behind him. "This fruit is ripe for the picking. Where are you?"

He looked back over his shoulder. The boy had disappeared. Uneasy now, the trader glanced around the clearing. Something was not right.

There was a scuffling sound in the undergrowth – and then a scream. The trader froze.

Suddenly a fist of gnarled claws shot out of the foliage and grabbed the fruit from the trader's hand. The man screamed as a hairy face

with bloodshot eyes emerged from behind the green leaves. Huge lips curled back to reveal thick, yellow teeth.

"Boy!" the trader croaked. "Run!"

Then his eyes darted to the jungle floor and what he saw made his blood run cold. All that remained of his companion were strips of torn

linen from the boy's tunic.

Slowly, the trader looked back at the Beast. It was too late for escape. He howled as a long, thick tail with a deadly claw on its tip flicked out and wrapped itself round his waist.

The trader's screams echoed around the jungle clearing. Then he was gone.

1

CROSSING THE WINDING RIVER

Tom guided his black stallion Storm inland, away from Avantia's western shore. Elenna sat behind him, her arms around his waist. Silver, Elenna's pet wolf, padded quietly alongside. Struggling with Zepha the Monster Squid had been their toughest challenge yet. If it hadn't been for Sepron, the great sea serpent and protector of Avantia's waters, they might never have defeated the Evil Beast.

Stored safely in Storm's saddlebag lay a magnificent golden helmet, shaped like the head of an eagle. It was the first piece from the great suit of Golden Armour, which gave magical powers to its rightful owner. The armour had belonged to the Master of the Beasts and had been destined to pass to Tom as a reward for completing his first Quest. Now it was Tom's fate to recover the six pieces, which had been stolen by the Dark Wizard Malvel and scattered across Avantia. But Malvel had charged six Evil Beasts with protecting each piece. Zepha had been the first, with the helmet as the prize. There were five more Beasts to overcome and five pieces of armour to collect.

But that was not all. For Malvel had taken more than the armour. He had kidnapped Aduro, King Hugo's wizard and Tom and Elenna's friend and protector.

"I'm worried about Aduro," Elenna said now.

"That's why we have to find and defeat this next Beast, Claw, whatever he is," said Tom. "We will soon find all six pieces of the armour and, when our Quest is complete, we will rescue Aduro. As he told us himself, there's no other way!"

Silver yapped in excitement, and

Storm tossed his fine head.

"Malvel may have Aduro," said Tom," but we still have Aduro's enchanted map. Let's see if it will tell us where we can find Claw."

They dismounted and Tom drew the parchment scroll from the saddlebag. As he unrolled it, the map sprang to life. The mountains of Avantia rose as high as his thumb and tiny waves crashed on the map's shores. Tom and Elenna shared a smile. No matter how many times they used the magical map, it never failed to amaze them.

Slowly the image on the map began to slide up, revealing new terrain in the south. The landscape grew greener. Suddenly a glowing red line appeared from Avantia's western shore and snaked down, past the Winding River, into a small patch of green in the south-east.

Elenna put her finger to the map, then started and pulled her hand away in surprise. It felt warm and damp.

"I have an idea where we might be headed," said Tom, frowning. "There's a place called the Dark Jungle in the south-east. The people of Avantia rarely go there."

"Why not?" Elenna asked.

"The Dark Jungle is dangerous as well as hot," Tom told her. "Strange creatures live in it. There are poisonous plants and spiders the size of your head. I've heard that if the heat and the insects don't kill you, the creatures will."

Elenna shuddered.

Tom studied the map more closely. Something was moving in the depths of the Dark Jungle. It glimmered, then disappeared again.

"Look," Tom said, showing Elenna the map. "Can you see? That tiny gold dot. Look closely."

"It's the chainmail!" Elenna said in excitement. "The next piece of the armour!"

Tom rolled up the map. "We're going to the Dark Jungle," he said. "There's no time to lose!"

Tom, Elenna, Storm and Silver headed further inland, towards the Winding River. With the sun on their backs and wonderful views of Avantia all around them, it was easy to forget the danger of their Quest.

They followed the road down into a green valley. Tom took out the map again and studied their position, tracing the red line towards the Dark Jungle.

When he had looked the first time, the tiny golden chainmail had been near the mouth of the jungle. Now it was deep among the trees.

Had Malvel moved it?

Tom's heart thumped.

Did he know they were coming?

They carried on. The road led deep into the valley. Soon Tom and Elenna could see the gleaming ribbon of

water that was the Winding River.
The riverbank twisted and turned
like a writhing snake, and the water
was turning gold in the late-afternoon
sun.

But the road stopped abruptly at
the river's edge and there was no sign
of a bridge. The water rushed past

them, wild and foaming. It looked dangerous.

Carefully, Tom took the golden helmet from the saddlebag. It shone in the sunlight as if it were made of fire. His heart beating fast, Tom raised it above his head and slowly pulled it down over his face.

At once, his eyesight sharpened. He could see every blade of grass along the riverbank and, when he looked downstream, he saw the river stretching away for miles. Everything was crystal clear.

"Can you see anything?" Elenna asked.

"I can see *everything*," Tom said in wonder. "It's amazing! But I can't see a bridge."

"The river twists away behind those trees," said Elenna, pointing upstream. "Perhaps there is a bridge somewhere out of sight."

As they followed the river, Tom began to feel worried. The light was fading rapidly now and he felt they had to cross the water before nightfall.

They rounded another twist in the river. Silver barked.

"There!" Elenna shouted.

At last, a bridge.

But it looked old. The planks were warped, rickety and broken in several places, and some were missing entirely, like teeth in an old witch's mouth. The water swirled below, white and furious.

"It won't take our weight if we cross together," said Tom, jumping from Storm. "But if we go one at a time, we might make it. Elenna, get Silver over first."

In three bounds, Silver was across. The bridge creaked and swayed, but stayed in one piece.

Tom gave Elenna an encouraging

nod as she stepped on to the bridge. One of the planks cracked and fell into the water as she leapt for the shore. But she made it.

"Come on, Storm," Tom coaxed, trying to sound confident. "You next."

But the stallion was spooked by the swirling water and refused to move.

Tom stepped on to the bridge, testing the plank with his weight. The twisted wood creaked under his feet, but didn't break.

"Come on, boy," Tom called softly, holding out his hand.

The stallion stepped forwards. The wooden slats groaned in protest and the bridge swayed. Storm rolled his eyes in terror, as Tom struggled to keep him calm and urge him forward.

A rotten plank snapped just as Storm's last back hoof lifted from it. Then the entire section of the bridge they had been standing on crumbled into the angry, churning water below.

"We need to lighten the load," Tom called over his shoulder to Elenna. Very slowly, he sank to his knees to spread his weight. Then he unfastened his helmet, shield and sword.

"Catch!"

The bridge groaned again as Tom threw everything towards Elenna. Now he had no magic to protect him, only his wits.

Tom edged forward but the planks splintered. He could only watch in

horror as the groaning bridge began
to fall away.

"Come on, Storm!" he shouted,
scrambling towards the shore.

But the stallion threw back his
head and whinnied in terror as the
bridge collapsed beneath him.

"No!" Elenna screamed from the riverbank.

But it was too late. Tom and Storm had fallen into the deadly water!

2

ORDEAL IN THE WATER

Tom felt himself being dragged under the surface. The water was cold and the current strong. He could sense Storm panicking and thrashing his legs. With a lunge, Tom grabbed hold of the stallion's reins.

Half-blinded and choking, he somehow broke the surface of the river. "Throw me my sword!" he shouted to Elenna.

The heavy sword flew through the air and plunged into the water beside him. Storm kicked wildly. With a mighty effort, Tom reached out and grabbed hold of the hilt before the sword sank out of sight. His lungs were burning

as he stabbed his sword into the
riverbank with all his might and
held on. The power of the current
and Storm's weight almost dragged
Tom away. But he kept his grip on
the sword, and the blade held fast in
the ground.

"Tom!" Elenna called, running to
the edge of the river and holding out
her hand.

He kicked hard, and felt solid
ground just in front of him. His feet
slithered through the mud, and the
water sucked at his legs. Grunting
with the effort, Tom grabbed
Elenna's outstretched hand. Then
he swung himself on to the bank
and collapsed on the grass, Storm's
soaking leather reins gripped in his

other fist. But the horse was still struggling in the wild water, his hooves flailing.

"Pull with me, Elenna," Tom shouted.

Silver ran up and down the bank, barking and whining, as Elenna put her arms around Tom's waist. Together they tried to drag Storm closer to the bank. But it was no good.

"Come on, Storm," Tom urged. His legs were trembling with exhaustion as he fell to his knees and gazed at his stallion.

Storm's eyes were wide and scared as the water rushed past him. He was beginning to lose the battle.

"Steady," Tom murmured, almost

as if he were talking to himself.
"Stay calm. Stay calm…"

He repeated the words over and
over again, clicking his tongue, and
gradually Storm's terrified eyes
focused on him again.

Then, one step at a time, the
stallion heaved himself through
the water. At last, with a final,
huge effort, he scrambled on to the
riverbank.

Tom threw his arms around his horse. "Well done, Storm," he gasped, burying his face in the stallion's damp neck. He could feel himself grinning. "You did it, boy."

Elenna fell on Storm's neck and hugged the stallion fiercely. "Oh, Storm," she murmured. "I thought we'd lost you."

Snorting and blowing, Storm quietened. He nuzzled Tom gently, as Elenna rushed to collect long grasses to dry the horse's flanks. They needed to get him dry and warm as quickly as possible.

As Tom unsaddled Storm and rubbed him with the grass, Elenna lit a camp fire. Then Tom draped a blanket around the exhausted stallion. Storm swayed on his feet, as if he were too tired to stand up for much longer. Then he sank gently to the ground beside the fire.

Quickly, Tom stripped off his wet clothes and wrapped himself in another blanket. His clothes would dry overnight beside the flames. Meanwhile, Silver brought Elenna a rabbit he had caught on the riverbank.

"Is the feast to your liking?" Tom joked, offering Elenna a piece of bread and cheese as the rabbit roasted in the embers of the fire.

Elenna tore into the bread. "It'll do," she said between mouthfuls, and smiled.

Later Tom and Elenna ate the

rabbit beside the crackling fire. The rushing sound of the water was comforting now.

"Let's hope we don't have any more water challenges for a while," Elenna said with a sigh.

Tom lay back and stared at the night sky overhead. It was dotted with bright stars, and the moon was almost full. His thoughts drifted to his father, Taladon, who had once undertaken a Beast Quest of his own. He wondered where he was now.

Then he realised that, at this moment, Elenna, Storm and Silver were the closest thing to a family that he had. He never wanted to risk losing any of them again.

3

INTO THE DARK JUNGLE

The morning dawned clear and still. To Tom's relief, Storm seemed rested and calm after his ordeal in the water. Tom and Elenna breakfasted on fresh fish that Elenna caught in the waters of the Winding River. Silver bounded away as they ate, returning with another plump rabbit for himself.

"Time to go," said Tom at last.

Elenna doused the fire and packed her belongings. Tom knew she was thinking about the Beast they were about to face. If he was honest, he was thinking about it as well. What sort of a creature would Claw be?

They soon found a road which led away from the Winding River. As they journeyed on, the valley walls grew steeper and the vegetation more lush. Silver ran on ahead, as clouds chased each other across the stripe of blue sky above their heads.

After a while the road dwindled to a stony track, potholed in places. It was clear that few people came this way. The thought made Tom feel uncomfortable. If the rumours about the Dark Jungle were true, what chance did they have of defeating Claw and finding the golden chainmail?

The stony track began to climb. Panting, Storm trudged up the steep incline, Silver padding quietly by his side. The sun beat down hard on Tom and Elenna's backs. The air felt close.

The track ended abruptly as they reached the top of a hill. Before them lay a sea of green trees. It stretched as far as the horizon.

"The Dark Jungle," Elenna said in awe. "It's bigger than I'd imagined."

The jungle was vast. Above the trees, the air shimmered with heat. The only way down to the jungle's edge was straight across a marshy stretch of ground. Mosquitoes whined though the air. Storm flicked his ears as the insects darted in to bite where they could.

Tom's heart raced with a mixture of fear and excitement as he clicked his tongue and urged Storm forward. Batting at the insects, they struggled on to the edge of the jungle.

Soon they were facing a dense wall of trees. Strange screeching sounds could be heard high in the canopy. The air was still and expectant.

"I don't like this," Elenna murmured.

Tom could feel Storm tensing beneath him. He shifted the shield on his arm, bringing it close to his chest. Silver was pacing uncomfortably, his tail low and his ears flattened to his head. It was impossible to ignore the feeling of menace that surrounded the Dark Jungle.

Taking out Aduro's map, Tom studied it once more. The golden dot of the chainmail had moved again. Now it looked very close to where they were standing. Tom squinted through the trees.

"We have no choice, Elenna," he said, rolling up the map. "We have to go in. We need to defeat all the Beasts and collect every piece of the Golden Armour before we can rescue Aduro."

Tom thought again about the kindly wizard. He swallowed.

"We have to rescue him," he said

firmly, and urged Storm forward.

The four Questers took their first steps into the Dark Jungle. Tom immediately noticed the stifling heat. It was hard to breathe and he felt the pressure on his lungs. Storm shook his head nervously, while Silver growled softly. Fleshy jungle plants hung all around them. The air was thick and sticky with their strange and powerful scents.

"I have never seen plants like these," Elenna said in wonder. She stretched out her hand to touch a red trumpet-shaped flower.

Immediately the flower snapped closed and, before Elenna could react, snake-like tendrils wrapped themselves around her arm.

"Tom!" she shrieked.

Tom pulled out his sword and slashed the tendrils away. "Touch nothing," he warned, glancing around. He half-expected to see Malvel himself, laughing from the treetops.

The air grew thicker and darker as they pressed on, and the ground became wetter. Soon Storm was wading cautiously through dark, stinking water, his hooves sliding in the mud, his nostrils flaring at the unfamiliar scents.

"It's all right," Tom soothed, and stroked his horse's mane.

Halfway across the swamp, Tom dismounted. He did not want to be responsible for Storm sinking into the uncertain ground. Elenna did the same and pressed ahead with Silver.

The water was unpleasantly warm and sucked at his legs. Gritting his teeth, Tom took Storm's reins and led the stallion gently onwards. His eyes darted around, checking for signs of the Beast.

Elenna was waiting for them on the far side of the swamp, Silver at her side. She was cutting away the leeches which had attached themselves to her flesh, then she did the same for Tom and Storm.

They moved on, wet and tired. At last, they emerged into a sun-dappled open space.

A group of chattering monkeys suddenly swung down through the vines. Silver barked furiously and Storm reared in surprise.

Tom and Elenna dived on to the jungle floor in fright.

"Stay down, Elenna!" Tom said, reaching for his sword.

Gibbering among themselves, the monkeys settled in a tree and began grooming each other. Sheepishly, Tom and Elenna got to their feet.

"That's the first and last time I'm ever going to be scared of a monkey," said Elenna with a nervous laugh.

They moved on, Tom using his sword to

slash through the damp green undergrowth.

Suddenly Elenna stopped. "Look," she said, pointing at a series of deep gashes in the tree trunks.

"Something has happened here," Tom said slowly, inspecting several huge chunks gouged out of the undergrowth. Torn branches littered the ground. Storm gave a high, anxious whinny.

Elenna picked up something limp and tattered. "A strip of linen," she said, turning it over in her hand.

There were several more strips of cloth scattered across the clearing. Tom and Elenna looked at each other. Even after facing seven Beasts, the sight of such destruction was unsettling. And the torn linen suggested something more sinister than ever before.

Tom took the piece of cloth. "What could have done this?" he said.

Just then they heard a rustling behind them. Tom and Elenna whirled around, as a claw that was bigger than both of their heads swiped at them from high up in the trees. It was attached to a long, furry tail.

Tom pushed Elenna out of the way, and they tumbled to the ground.

A chill settled on Tom's heart.
It was the Beast. And now the
Beast knew they were here.

1

CLAW ON THE ATTACK

Tom peered up into the canopy of trees. It was almost impossible to see anything against the glare of the sun. Leaves rustled and brushed against each other. The Dark Jungle sounded as if it were laughing at its visitors.

A stench of old meat and sweat drifted down through the branches, stronger than the sickly scents of the jungle flowers.

Tom peered up again. But it was no use. The Beast was too high up.

"If only I could see more clearly," he said, frustrated. Then he remembered the golden helmet!

Quickly he pulled it from Storm's saddlebag and put it on, gazing up into the treetops again. Now he was able to see the gorgeous greens and vivid colours of the highest point of the jungle.

Then Tom spotted the Beast. He felt his eyes widen in disbelief.

Claw was an enormous monkey. His chest was as wide as Storm was long, and his limbs were thicker than some of the tree trunks around them. He sat hunched among the branches, a hideous creature with a lethal-looking claw at the tip of his long, snake-like tail. Huge, hairy brown arms, legs and feet ended in vicious, curved claws. His face was covered in matted brown hair, but

his squashed snout was hairless. Drool hung in ropes from his long teeth. And his fierce yellow eyes were trained directly on Tom.

He knew they had to run. There was no choice.

"Jump up here, Elenna!" Tom cried, leaping on to Storm and throwing the helmet back into the safety of the saddlebag.

Elenna flung herself into the saddle behind him, scrabbling for a grip, and Tom wheeled the stallion around so hard that Storm reared and nearly fell.

But before the stallion could take them to safety, a torrent of twigs,branches and vines plunged down from the canopy, knocking Tom

and Elenna from the saddle. Claw
gave a screech of triumph.

Tom tried to struggle to his feet
but the weight of the twisted vines
was pressing down on him, like
an enormous tangled net. Storm
neighed in terror and Silver snarled.

"I can't move!" Elenna cried.

The more they twisted, the more
tightly the vines drew around
them. The stench of the Beast was
everywhere. Tom's arms were pinned
down; he couldn't reach his sword.

Claw screeched again. Then, to
Tom's horror, the Beast's long, clawed
tail swung down and plucked Elenna
into the air, ripping the tangled vines
away from her with ease.

"Tom!" screamed Elenna.

"No!" Tom cried. He fought to escape, but there was nothing he could do.

Elenna kicked and yelled, as the Beast pulled her up into the trees. Her arms flailed, hitting out uselessly at her captor. "Tom!" she screamed again. "Help me!"

Then there was a sudden awful silence. Where had the Beast taken her?

With a snarl, Silver ripped himself clear with his teeth, before tearing at the vines around Tom.

"That's it, boy!" Tom shouted, struggling to free his arms. "Nearly there!"

At last, he could move his arms. Bursting free, he withdrew his sword and thrust it fiercely into the air.

"While there's blood in my veins," he vowed, "I'll save my friend!"

Quickly, he cut away the vines that still bound Storm's legs. The stallion waited patiently as Tom tugged him loose.

Claw had left a trail of destruction

in his wake – broken branches and scattered leaves on the jungle floor – so it would be easy to follow him. But Tom needed to approach the Beast with care if he was to save Elenna.

Picking up the scent of his mistress, Silver threw back his head and started to howl.

"No!" Tom cried, running to the wolf. He patted the animal's thick fur and shushed him. Noise was the last thing Tom needed.

But it was too late. Behind him, Tom heard a telltale rustling. He looked over his shoulder, hooking a protective arm around Silver.

The Beast's huge shadow spread across the clearing. Claw was back, high in the trees once more. There was no sign of Elenna. Where was she?

Tom tensed as the clawed tail flew down through the branches once again. He dived out of the way, but the claw violently slapped Silver and Storm to one side, and Tom lost sight of them. He hoped desperately that they were all right, and concentrated on the branches, waiting for the tail to reappear.

It lashed towards him suddenly.

Tom ducked, desperate to evade the cruel claw at its tip. The Beast remained in the trees. It was impossible for Tom to see more than his tail.

Claw gibbered and whirled his tail

again. This time, Tom reached out and grabbed hold of it. He held on tightly.

"Come down, you coward!" Tom yelled, tugging at the Beast in an effort to bring him crashing to the ground.

The great monkey simply lifted his tail. Yanked off his feet, Tom went flying through the air.

Tom clung on with all his strength, as Claw's tail whipped and thrashed around. The Beast roared and leapt from tree to tree. Tom swung beneath him, jagged twigs and branches tearing at his clothes. The breath was knocked out of him as the Beast slammed him into trees and dragged him through curtains of vines that scratched his face.

This was it. There was no way out.

He wasn't going to escape from the Dark Jungle alive!

5

FALLING

Tom couldn't hold on much longer.
His clothes were torn to shreds.
His arms and legs were black with
bruises. He knew he had to let go.

Timing it as best he could, Tom
released his hold on the Beast's
tail and plummeted downwards.
Stretching out for the nearest tree,
his fingers snagged on a branch and
he swung there, breathless but safe.

Above him Claw stood up, thumped his vast chest and shrieked at the sky. The treetops shook.

His hands scratched and numb, Tom nearly lost his grip on the branch, but managed to wrap his legs around the tree trunk. For the first time, he could see all of Claw, as the Beast swung from tree to tree above him. The strange movement of the golden dot on Aduro's map suddenly made sense.

The chainmail was draped around Claw's neck.

Tom gasped with wonder at the sight. The piece of armour shimmered magically. The links seemed too fine to be made of metal, and made Tom think of golden silk, knotted into a pattern that sparkled in the light.

Suddenly Claw dropped down through the trees and lunged at Tom

again. The Beast's cruel lips were drawn back, revealing his horrible, grinning fangs. Tom grabbed his sword and fought as hard as he could, but it was almost impossible to keep a grip on the tree while he swung his blade. The trees weren't his natural home. Claw was at a huge advantage.

The clawed tail shot towards him once again. This time, it knocked Tom's sword out of his hand. Tom watched in horror as his weapon spiralled down to the ground and out of sight. Now he was defenceless.

He risked a glance at the jungle floor. It seemed a long way down, but his position on the tree trunk was dangerous. He shifted his shield further on to his back, trying to get a better grip on the branch.

Think, Tom, he told himself fiercely.

Then it came to him.

Onto his shield was fixed the eagle's feather that Arcta the Mountain Giant had given him. It protected him from falling from great heights.

Pulling his shield from his back, he held it above him.

Then he took a deep breath and jumped.

Vines and branches whistled past, but Tom felt the power of the shield protecting him. His fall was slowing.

Even so, he hit the ground hard, the breath knocked out of him.

Within moments, he was buried in the undergrowth. To his relief, his sword lay nearby. He stretched out a hand and grabbed it.

Claw shrieked once more, the sound echoing around the jungle. Then silence fell. It seemed that the Beast had given him up for dead.

Tom lay as still as he could, the comforting weight of the sword in his hand. His first thoughts were for Storm and Silver. He hadn't seen the two of them since the Beast had knocked them aside with his tail. Had they survived? His heart lurched as he glanced around.

Then he heard Storm neigh. The ground beneath him trembled as the stallion cantered towards him with

Silver close at his heels.

Storm nudged him and whinnied.

"Hush," Tom whispered, reaching up and stroking Storm's nose. "I'm all right."

He peered through the leaves over his head. There was nothing in the canopy above him. Tom climbed to his feet. He could hardly believe that he had no broken limbs.

He looked at his shield and offered silent thanks to Avantia's great Beasts who had given him their tokens of power, now set deep into the wooden face of the shield: Ferno's dragon-scale protected him from heat, Sepron's tooth from onrushing water, and Nanook's bell from extreme cold. Tagus's horseshoe fragment gave him extra speed and Epos's golden talon healed wounds. And, of course, Arcta's eagle feather, which protected him from great heights, had just saved his life.

Hacking his way free from the undergrowth was almost as difficult as freeing himself from the vines. The ferns of the Dark Jungle were thick and strong, and curled around him.

Then Tom felt something tickling his leg. He looked down.

A snake was coiled around his knee. Its green-brown skin gleamed in the dim jungle light. Every now and again, a thin black tongue flickered and was gone again. Its yellow eyes were fixed on Tom.

Without taking his eyes off the snake, Tom knocked the creature into the air with the tip of his sword and sliced through its body. The snake's scaly coils twitched and fell to the ground in two pieces. Tom sighed with relief.

Silver pressed his nose to the ground. His ears pricked and he whined. He had picked up Elenna's scent again!

Tom leapt into Storm's saddle. It was time for battle.

We're coming, Elenna! he

thought. *Just hold on!*

Silver took off, following the scent. Broken branches dangled from the trees above them as Tom and Storm galloped through the jungle after the wolf. The Beast had cut a path through the canopy that was easy to follow.

Stumbling and slipping, they raced past trunks as thick as ten men. Storm darted between trees and beneath vines, taking sharp turns and following the wolf. Alert for signs of danger, Tom watched the trees and clutched his sword.

It wasn't long before the tangle of trees cleared a little. Silver bounded forward and Storm tossed his head as Tom pressed his heels into the stallion's flanks, encouraging him to gallop faster.

But something was wrong with the path in front of them. The land ahead seemed to be falling away. Storm stiffened as Tom desperately reined him in.

"Silver!" Tom cried. "Look out!"

The wolf twisted his body sharply. But it was too late. Tom watched in horror as Silver went skidding over the edge – and out of sight!

6

INTO THE VOLCANO

Tom flung himself off Storm and
ran to the edge of the precipice.
An enormous hole in the ground
lay before him. Tom felt a tremor
run through his body. He had seen
something like this before, when he
had freed Epos the Flame Bird from
Malvel's curse. Only that chasm had
been blazing with lava and smoke.

This was rich with plant life.

It was the crater of a vast, extinct volcano.

Tom remembered the horrors of his battle to free Epos. He had come close to falling into the boiling lava because he had moved too near the crater's border, where the ground was loose. This time, he sank to his knees and crawled to the edge.

Far below, the heart of the crater was as dark as night. Trees grew tall, reaching up towards the blue sky, desperate for light. It was almost impossible to make out the ground beneath the luxuriant canopy of leaves.

There was no way that Silver could have survived the fall.

But then Tom caught sight of the wolf's silvery pelt. His heart leapt with joy as he saw Silver crouched below him, on a nearly invisible ledge beneath the lip of the crater. Somehow the wolf had stopped himself from falling any further.

Silver stood on his back legs as Tom reached out to him, nosing thankfully at Tom's hand. The ledge was at an awkward angle, tucked underneath the overhang where Tom lay. Reaching down, Tom sank his fingers into Silver's thick pelt and grasped hold of the loose folds of skin around the wolf's neck. He heaved with all his might, and the wolf scrambled out.

"Good boy," Tom murmured,

rubbing Silver's head. He felt faint with relief.

The wolf suddenly pulled away from Tom. He ran to the edge of the precipice again, pacing nervously near the edge, sniffing at the air. He growled softly and looked at Tom with his brown eyes.

"What is it?" Tom said, his heart filling with hope.

Silver whined and paced close to the crater, stopping just short of the edge. Stones broke away and bounced down the sheer slope, out of sight.

The golden helmet would help Tom see what Silver had scented. He ran to Storm and lifted the helmet from the saddlebag once more. Then he placed it on his head and gazed back down at the crater.

He could see brightly coloured beetles and sleeping snakes, and every leaf was pinpoint clear. Tom's eyes swept the ground again. Then, through a crack in the canopy, he spotted Elenna in the gloom at the heart of the crater itself.

She was sitting on the ground, her head in her arms. Scattered around her were piles of gleaming white bones, picked clean. It was Claw's lair, the place he brought his victims. Elenna looked unhurt, but she was trapped at the bottom of the crater.

Tom's head was whirling. He had to defeat Claw and get the chainmail – only by completing the suit of

Golden Armour piece by piece could
he rescue Aduro. But first, he needed
to save Elenna.

"You can do this!" Tom told
himself. "Take it one step at a time."

He glanced around, looking for

the Beast. He didn't want Claw to know he had found Elenna. Then he gave a long, low whistle to catch his friend's attention. The Beast was less likely to hear him that way.

Elenna looked up. The thick canopy of leaves was blocking her view of Tom. He whistled again. Getting to her feet, Elenna moved to a piece of clear ground – and grinned with relief when she saw him.

Tom placed a finger on his lips, warning her to stay quiet. He could smell Claw's stench; the Beast wasn't far away. Shadows danced on the ground from the branches high above, playing tricks on Tom's eyes. He whirled about, his eyes darting from shadow to shadow. Where was the giant monkey?

At last, Tom spotted him. High in the canopy above Tom's head, the Beast's long, clawed tail swung lazily back and forth. It looked as if the creature was asleep. The chainmail glimmered and clinked around his neck. The sound made Tom think of tiny bells. His heart quickened. The armour seemed to call out to him, shining softly in the sunlight. Tom hesitated, glancing back at the crater.

Elenna first, he thought.

He looked at the vertical walls of the precipice. There was no way down or up. And it was too deep for any of the nearby vines to reach the bottom. Tom was at a loss.

He had no idea how to rescue Elenna.

A hissing sound made him look down. Elenna was gesturing something. At last, Tom realised what she wanted – her bow and arrow!

Tom began a careful sweep of the ground where Claw had dragged Elenna to his lair. Silver kept watch at the mouth of the crater while Storm quietly cropped the grass.

At last, Tom spotted the familiar leather quiver holding Elenna's arrows. Beside it lay her bow. They hadn't fallen into the crater. But they were teetering dangerously close to the edge.

Tom reached for the weapons, but they were just too far from his grasp. He couldn't creep any closer to the edge, or he would tumble over and all would be lost. He watched in dismay as a gust of wind caused the quiver to see-saw gently over the chasm. There wasn't a moment to lose!

Wrapping one hand around a nearby gum tree, Tom leaned as far as he dared towards the weapons. His fingertips brushed the quiver, but he wasn't close enough to grasp it. He uncurled his fingers slightly from the gum tree and dug his toes into the damp ground. A little further...just a little...

Suddenly Tom felt his fingers

slip from the gum tree. His toes scrabbled for grip, but it was hopeless. He felt himself toppling and there was nothing he could do.

Tom was falling. The Quest was lost.

Aduro! Tom thought. *Aduro, I'm sorry…*

But then, just as he was about to tip over the edge of the crater, something grabbed his leg and held him fast. Tom glanced over his shoulder to see Silver gripping his trouser leg in his powerful jaws.

Grasping the bow and arrows firmly in his hand, Tom rolled back from the edge of the crater with a hammering heart.

"Thank you, Silver," he whispered,

throwing his arms around the wolf's strong neck. "What would I do without you?"

He tied the bow and quiver of arrows together with a vine and threw them down to Elenna. Without a word, she took the arrows in her quiver, fitted them to her bow, and began shooting them into the walls of the crater.

Everything became clear as Tom watched where the arrows fell. They had formed a ladder up the crater wall that she could climb to safety.

Tom fell back with a gasp of relief. The ground was cool under him. He knew how lucky he was to have such a quick-thinking companion on this Quest. Elenna would climb out of the sleeping volcano and then they would face Claw.

Together.

FACING THE BEAST

When he had caught his breath, Tom glanced up into the canopy again. He was still wearing the helmet and could see that Claw remained sleeping, his limbs hanging like thick hairy ropes from the branch overhead, the golden chainmail glinting in the sun. They were still safe – although there was no way of telling for how long.

He wriggled back to the edge of
the crater and watched as Elenna
stepped up on to the first arrow. It
bent slightly beneath her weight, and
she struggled to keep her balance.

Tom ran to a nearby tree and
cut down a length of vine with his
sword. He looped it around a tree
trunk and threw the other end to
Elenna. It reached halfway down.
If she could just get there, he and
Silver could pull her up the rest of
the way.

Elenna nodded gratefully up at
Tom, understanding what he was
trying to do. But first she had to get
to the vine.

Tom looked on with admiration
as his friend grasped the arrow

above her head then climbed on to the arrow just below, repeating this movement until she had reached the vine. Each time she took a step up, she reached down to retrieve the arrow she had left behind.

Silver ran back and forth along the mouth of the crater. To Tom's relief, the wolf seemed to know that he should be silent.

Soon Elenna reached the vine and grabbed the end of it. Together, Tom and Silver pulled the vine up the side of the crater. Tom wanted to shout for joy as he felt the grasp of his friend's warm palm.

"We did it!" he whispered fiercely, as he and Elenna swiftly embraced.

They were back together!

But now it was time to face the Beast and retrieve the golden chainmail.

"If I climb into the trees," Tom said in a low voice, "I might take Claw by surprise. It's the only advantage we have."

Elenna nodded, her eyes wide and fearful.

Tom walked to a nearby tree and tested it with his weight.

It was the wrong thing to do.

The tree groaned and started to sway. Then, to Tom's horror, its roots began to rise up from the soft ground.

"It's dead!" Elenna gasped, backing away as the tree began to topple.

Tom grabbed Storm's bridle, Elenna grasped Silver's pelt, and they all ran clear as the tree thundered to the ground.

The sound boomed around the Dark Jungle.

Then they heard a scream from the canopy.

Claw was awake.

"We just lost our advantage," Elenna panted as she ran.

Tom watched with awe as the Beast leapt from tree to tree, screeching and beating his chest.

"I still have to fight him, Elenna," he said. "I have to get the chainmail."

"I know," Elenna replied unhappily. "But be careful!"

Tom tucked the golden helmet back into Storm's saddlebag, then gave Elenna his shield. "Use it to protect yourself," he said, setting foot on the sturdiest tree he could see.

Soon he was climbing high into the canopy, his sword swinging awkwardly by his side. Above him, Claw chattered in fury, lashing out

with his tail. One hairy brown claw
was holding on to the chainmail. The
Beast had realised what Tom wanted
from him.

Tom ducked behind branches as
the Beast's razor-sharp tail whistled
towards him. Leaves and twigs
rained down on the jungle floor.

The tree he was climbing shook and shuddered. Grimly, Tom kept scrambling up, then tucked himself into the cleft of a branch and pulled out his sword, swinging it hard as, once again, the cruel claw whirled towards him.

Then came a stroke of pure luck: the base of the branch on which Claw was standing broke away from the tree. Screeching, the Beast fell through the leaves in a flurry of matted fur and thrashing limbs, his face contorted with rage.

But as he fell, he lashed out at Tom's branch.

Tom's heart lurched as the branch splintered beneath him. Instinctively he reached for his shield – and remembered too late that he had given it to Elenna.

Tom fell after the giant monkey, his

arms and legs flailing, and landed on a bed of broken branches.

On the ground, an arm's length from him, Claw was lurching wildly from side to side, roaring with anger, and making a clumsy retreat to the nearest tree trunk. But as soon as he leapt on to the tree, his agility and strength seemed to return.

Frustrated and exhausted, Tom prepared to follow. But before he could move, Elenna grabbed hold of him.

"Tom!" she said, her eyes alight. "Did you see how Claw couldn't balance on the ground?"

"I thought he had been injured in the fall," said Tom, as he gazed up at the canopy. "But he seems as strong as ever. Elenna, I don't know how I'm going to do this."

"No," Elenna said. "He wasn't injured. It was his curved claws. They gave him no grip on the forest floor. You can't defeat him *off* the ground – we've both seen how he swings through the trees as if he has wings. But if you can somehow get him *on* the ground, then the fight will be even."

Tom glanced up at the Beast. Elenna was right. His curved claws were perfectly adapted for swinging among the treetops. Walking on the ground was another matter.

But how could they coax Claw down to the jungle floor? It was impossible!

Tom was exhausted now. He groaned. There was no way he could do this on his own.

Dimly he heard Aduro's voice in his head: "Don't give up hope, Tom. Have you forgotten the help you have with you?"

Yes! he thought. *I'm not alone. I have the great Beasts of Avantia on my side.*

Without Sepron the Sea Serpent's help, Tom knew that they would never have retrieved the golden helmet from Zepha the Monster Squid. It was time to call on the help of another Beast. And Tom knew exactly who he needed this time. The thought both thrilled and terrified him. For this Beast was one of the mightiest in all of Avantia.

Ferno the Fire Dragon.

8

FERNO RETURNS

Tom seized his shield from Elenna and quickly rubbed the dragon-scale set deep into its surface. He felt a rush of exhilaration when he heard Ferno's roar. It filled the air with heat. The sky above the jungle shimmered. Creatures in the darkness of the jungle shrieked in fear and fled.

The mighty dragon of Avantia

soared over the jungle canopy, creating a ring of fire in the top branches of the nearby trees, his bluish-black leathery wings beating hard, his eyes glowing red in his face.

Exhilarated at the sight of their old friend, Elenna and Tom clung together and watched as smoke began to fill the already stifling jungle.

The air darkened. Branches crackled. Trees exploded.

Claw was being smoked out!

The Beast screamed his defiance at the dragon. He swung from a branch with one massive arm and beat his chest with the other. But it was a useless display. Ferno swooped again. The blazing fires gleamed on his polished scales. Claw bellowed and fled through the canopy.

Ferno flew above the giant monkey, following his progress through the branches. The dragon's tail struck the trees and brought them crashing down in the giant monkey's path.

Screeching parrots fluttered into the air, their vivid colours dulled by the smoke. Everywhere, the tops of the trees were burning.

"Go, Ferno!" Elenna screamed.

Tom willed the dragon on with all his heart.

Claw couldn't fight much longer. The Beast was struggling for breath, his chest heaving, as he held his great curved claws over his head, batting uselessly at the smoke. It was everywhere, curling and billowing through the sky. The only place that remained smoke-free was the jungle floor. In desperation, Claw dropped to the ground, snarling.

As soon as the Beast landed, Tom struck, his sword flashing, his shield protecting his head. Claw stumbled, trying to get away, but his clawed feet weren't quick enough. Tom gave chase, leaping through the undergrowth. The Beast hobbled pitifully, stumbling and groaning.

Elenna unleashed a volley of arrows. Claw howled in pain.

"Go, Silver!" she shouted.

The wolf nipped at the Beast's legs in a whirl of silver fur, and Storm joined the fight, his hooves sharp and deadly.

With the help of his friends, Tom closed the gap between himself and the Beast.

Claw was cornered.

The giant monkey curled back his horrible lips. The sight of his

putrid yellow fangs was terrifying.
Tom thrust hard with his sword,
aiming for the clasp on the golden
chainmail, which still hung around
the Beast's neck. He had to get it –
whatever it took.

But Claw was not helpless after
all. The great clawed tail slashed
through the air and flicked him
away. Tom tried again. And again
the Beast's tail knocked him away.
No matter how Tom approached, he
could not reach the chainmail with
his sword.

Desperate to distract the giant
monkey, Tom whistled sharply
for Storm. As the stallion crashed
through the foliage, Claw reared
back and Tom seized his chance. He

raced up close, moving his shield to his back, and leapt onto a nearby branch to raise himself level with the Beast's neck. Then, in the blink of an eye, he slid the tip of his sword into the chainmail's clasp and pulled. It half-opened.

Then the giant monkey's eyes flicked back to Tom and he lunged forward, wrapping his tail around Tom's waist. Tom stared with panic into the Beast's foul face as he felt himself being lifted into the air, his feet dangling above the ground. The tail's grip grew tighter as Tom struggled. He could feel his insides being crushed. His sword arm was pinned to his side, the weapon useless. The Beast prepared to leap

once again into the few remaining
trees that weren't yet burning.

"No!" Tom bellowed helplessly.
Then he heard Storm whinnying a
high-pitched challenge and turned
to see Elenna galloping towards him

on the black stallion, a splintered
tree branch in her hand. She aimed
the sharp tip of the branch at
Claw, and hurled it like a javelin. It
slammed into the half-open clasp on
the chainmail and loosened it still
further.

Claw's grip slackened and Tom
crashed back onto the jungle floor,
gulping deep breaths. There was
no time to check for injuries. Every
second counted.

Claw had dropped from the trees
again. Screaming at Tom, the hideous
Beast's tail whipped through the air.

"Ferno!" Tom shouted in
desperation, holding his shield above
his head.

The huge, scaly head of the fire

dragon darted down through the trees. Tom caught a glimpse of a blood-red eye. A jet of fire plumed from Ferno's mouth, bounced off the shield and hurtled towards Claw.

Like lightning, the giant monkey pulled back its tail and leapt back, gibbering in fear, as Ferno's flames consumed the ground in front of him. All around, the trees were burning fiercely. The shield protected Tom from heat, but he and his friends would soon be choked by the smoke.

"Again, Ferno!" Tom called, as his eyes stung and watered in the thick grey air.

Ferno roared, and there was another jet of bright flame. Elenna screamed. Tom almost fell backwards as he felt the force of the fire hurtle into the shield and change direction – straight towards the Beast.

9

VICTORY

Claw screeched, lurching away from the flames. There was nowhere left for him to go. The trees all around were burning, opening great charred gaps to the sky. The Beast fell to his knees. Tom threw himself at Claw's exposed neck and tore open the loosened clasp. At last, the golden chainmail slithered to the ground.

Ferno's roar shook the jungle.

One last column of fire, as wide as a tree trunk, blasted into the ground, hiding Claw behind a thick black cloud of smoke.

Stiffly, Tom reached for his sword again, ready to protect everything that he held dear.

The smoke began to clear. But where the great shaggy body of Claw should have been, something extraordinary met Tom's eyes.

A group of small, excitable monkeys were clustered together on the ground. They chattered, jumped into the lower branches of the unburnt trees, and happily groomed each other.

Where had the Beast gone?

Elenna looked as puzzled as Tom

felt. He gazed again at the empty space where Claw had cowered just a few seconds earlier. Then he stared back at the trees where the monkeys were sitting. He'd never seen anything quite like it before.

Then he realised it was all over. He collapsed to his knees, his lungs suddenly raw. Dimly he heard Elenna's voice.

"Tom!" she called. "Tom, you've done it!"

Ferno gave a piercing cry. Tom looked up. Above the burnt wreckage of the Dark Jungle, the vast wings of the dragon were beating.

"Thank you, Ferno," he whispered.

The dragon cried again, a sweet but fierce sound that Tom knew he would never forget. As Tom watched, he swooped away. Soon Ferno was no more than a black speck in the distance.

The next thing he saw was Elenna's face, grimy and bright with triumph.

"The chainmail, Tom!" she said. "It's yours!"

Climbing slowly to his feet, Tom stumbled over to the golden chainmail, the second piece of the precious armour. It was warm to the touch. He lifted it up, almost staggering at its weight. For a moment, he panicked. It was too heavy. He would never be able to lift it over his shoulders.

But as he did, the links slithered into place. Immediately, Tom became

aware of a magic pulse in his chest,
and the chainmail became as light
as a feather. Energy surged into
his tired muscles. He felt as brave
as a lion.

He looked at Elenna, who was
standing in the clearing with Storm
and Silver at her side. "Extra
strength of heart," he murmured,
stroking the chainmail. "The helmet

gives me sharper sight, and the chainmail makes me feel as if I could face any battle."

Elenna grinned. "Well done, Tom."

"I would never have called Ferno if you hadn't suggested that we had to fight Claw on the ground," Tom admitted.

"Hey," said Elenna, looking pleased. "I always knew I was the brains in this team."

Storm whinnied softly and pushed at Tom's hand. Tom stroked the stallion's dusty black coat, as Silver lay panting at Elenna's feet. Then he took off the chainmail and laid it gently across Storm's back. Tiredness seeped back into his muscles. "Now I could sleep for a week," he said. "But we still have four more pieces of armour to find, and four more Beasts to defeat. And Aduro…"

His voice trailed away. Soberly, Elenna met his gaze. Was King Hugo's wizard still alive? Was he holding out against Malvel's evil magic?

"We must leave this place,"Tom said. "We have to finish the Quest as quickly as we can so that we can rescue Aduro."

They began walking back the way they had come. Everything looked different, blackened and twisted by the force of Ferno's fire.

Soon they reached the thick green trees in the heart of the Dark Jungle. Ferno's flames had not touched this place. They moved slowly through the maze of plants and vines. Monkeys, small and unthreatening, chattered and swung through the branches above them.

"Watch out for snakes," Tom warned Elenna, remembering the snake he had killed. "They are everywhere."

Suddenly there was a strange thickening in the air.

"You'll have to watch out for more than that," came a mocking voice.

Tom gasped. He reached for his sword as a shimmering image of Malvel appeared against the canopy of leaves above them.

"We have two pieces of the Golden Armour, Malvel!" Tom shouted defiantly. "We defeated Claw! It won't be long before we find you and rescue Aduro – and then there will be nothing you can do."

"You will not be so sure of yourself when you meet the next evil Beast – Soltra," said Malvel.

"Where is Aduro?" Tom said challengingly.

Malvel laughed, a sneering sound

that echoed around the jungle. His image faded. In its place, Tom saw the great jungle crater they had left behind. Lying among the white animal bones was a scrap of blue cloth.

"Aduro's cloak is blue," said Elenna, her voice filled with anger. "What have you done with him, Malvel? If you have harmed him…"

The sound of Malvel's laughter filled the air once more as the image of the crater receded, and Tom felt something brush past him. He whirled around, but could see nothing.

"Good luck," the voice of Malvel whispered in his ear. It felt like the cold touch of a bat's wing. "You and

your team of nobodies. When you see
what still lies in store on this Quest,
you'll need it…"

Tom gripped his sword, feeling the
comforting weight of his shield on
his back. He remembered the golden
helmet in Storm's saddlebag and
glanced at the golden chainmail that
lay across the stallion's broad back.
They were not alone. The Beasts
of Avantia were on their side, and

with every Evil Beast he defeated
he gained one more piece of the
precious armour. His powers were
growing.

"We'll be ready!" he vowed,
thrusting his sword into the air.
"Whatever it takes, Malvel, while
there's blood in my veins, we will
defeat you!"

CONGRATULATIONS, YOU HAVE COMPLETED THIS QUEST!

At the end of each chapter you were awarded a special gold coin. The QUEST in this book was worth an amazing 10 coins.

Look at the Beast Quest totem picture inside the back cover of this book to see how far you've come in your journey to become

MASTER OF THE BEASTS.

The more books you read, the more coins you will collect!

Do you want your own Beast Quest Totem?
1. Cut out and collect the coin below
2. Go to the Beast Quest website
3. Download and print out your totem
4. Add your coin to the totem
www.beastquest.co.uk/totem

Don't miss the next exciting Beast Quest book, SOLTRA THE STONE CHARMER!

Read on for a sneak peek...

CHAPTER ONE

HOMEWARD BOUND

"At last!" gasped Tom as he pushed past a branch and found himself gazing out over open countryside.

"Thank goodness!" said Elenna from behind him. "I was beginning to think the Dark Jungle went on for ever."

They stepped out into the cool of the late afternoon, exhausted and glad to be free of the dark, sultry heat.

Ahead of them, the land sloped downwards in grassy terraces to a wide, winding river that rushed through deep stony banks. Tom took one final glance back into the sinister jungle, thinking about his battle with Claw the Giant Monkey, and remembering how he had just managed to snatch the golden chainmail from the Beast.

Silver, Elenna's faithful wolf, and Storm, Tom's noble stallion, emerged from the jungle, too. Silver bounded and barked joyfully, and Storm neighed and pranced.

"They're glad to be out in the open," Elenna said. "Can we camp for the night down by the river? I could catch us some fish for our supper."

Tom looked thoughtfully at her and sighed.

"What's wrong?" she asked.

"I was thinking about Aduro," he replied. "I'm worried about what Malvel might have done to him."

The Dark Wizard had kidnapped their friend and protector, Aduro – Avantia's Good Wizard. Malvel had appeared to them in a vision after Tom's defeat of Claw, showing them torn strips of Aduro's blue cloak.

Is he even still alive? Tom

wondered.

But whatever fate had befallen Aduro, Tom knew that he still had to fulfil his Quest and unite the six parts of the Golden Armour that Malvel had stolen and scattered across the kingdom. Aduro had told them it was the only way they could rescue him. Unless they succeeded, Avantia would never be safe from the six Evil Beasts set loose by Malvel.

Read
SOLTRA THE STONE CHARMER
to find out more!

Discover the new Beast Quest mobile game fro

Available free on iOS and Android

  amazon.com

Guide Tom on his Quest to free the Good Beasts
of Avantia from Malvel's evil spells.

Battle the Beasts, defeat the minions,
unearth the secrets and collect
rewards as you journey through the
Kingdom of Avantia.

DOWNLOAD THE APP TO BEGIN
THE ADVENTURE NOW!